Tang

MW01129942

The Little Turtle Who Was Afraid to Go to School

© 2015, Danielle R. Lindner
CreateSpace Publishing Company

ISBN-13: 978-1519300003
ISBN-10: 151930000X

Tango the Turtle was just turning four
He lived near the beach and played by the shore

1

He always had fun spending his day
Knowing that mom was a few feet away

2

Just mommy and me Tango would say
As he slowly meandered the long day away

Mom was always there right by his side
Digging the sand or riding the tide

But then one morning she did something new
She packed up a lunch, a change of clothes too

Tango she said, today is the day
I'll go to work and you'll go to play

6

You'll go to school, to learn and make friends
And together, we'll be, when the day finally ends

School Tango said, without you all day?
No Tango said, mommy don't go away!

8

School is such fun, you'll learn to read and to draw
You will learn how to share, count to ten on your claws

You will have loving teachers who hug you all day

Who help you with snack and find toys to play

12

And while you are there
I'll be just down the way
Doing the things that moms do all day

I'll get dinner done so its ready at five

Water the plants so I know they will thrive

15

Clean out the closet and go to the store
Pick up the dirty clothes from the floor

I'll pack dads suitcase for his short business trip
There are things to recycle and coupons to clip

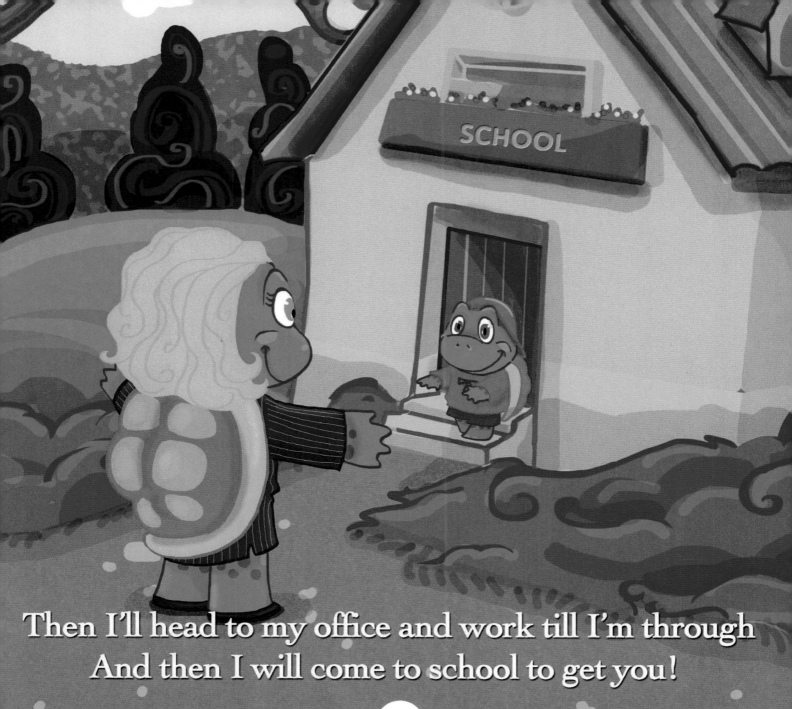

Then I'll head to my office and work till I'm through
And then I will come to school to get you!

And during the time that I am away
Your job will be to learn and to play

I will be calling a client at ten
And you will be having a snack about then

I have a meeting at three and at four

You have to paint and go play outdoors

But at the end of the day
One thing is true
No matter the day,
I'll always get you

23

And one day it will happen
You won't even believe
That you'll beg me to stay
You won't want to leave

24

And that's just what happened
To mommy's dismay
Tango said, mommy, please can I stay

Just one more minute
I want to finish my art,
and show you the blocks I made into a heart

26

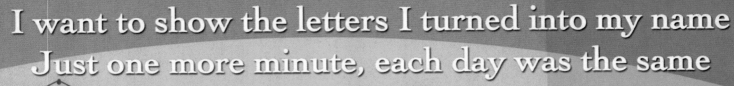

I want to show the letters I turned into my name
Just one more minute, each day was the same

Tango was scared to leave mommy for school
But soon he was happy and thought it was cool
Mom does her job and I do mine
She always came back, it was all fine

28

Mom missed Tango during her day
But she knew he was happy, he was ok
And Tango missed mommy at school sometimes too
But he always found something fun he could do!

Danielle Lindner is a member of the SCBWI (Society for Children's Book Writers & Illustrators) and a certified Early Educational and Elementary Teacher.

Always having a view to a career in education, Danielle gained an M.A. in Teaching and Elementary Education (Hons.), from Fairleigh Dickinson University in 1997. She has worked as a teacher, trainer and educator for over 19 years in both public and private educational institutions.

She is the Founder of The London Day School™ Preschool and Kindergarten Enrichment Academies. The London Day School™ was created by Ms. Lindner who saw a need for an enriching, challenging and socially engaging program for young children, that focuses on providing a scaffolding approach to learning and a strong character education curriculum for all students.

Ms.Lindner's other books include, Sofia the Snail - The little snail that was afraid of the dark, Arabelle - The bat with the most wonderful pink glasses, Rupert - The little puppy who ran out of tears, Betsie Bee - The little bee who learned how to share and care in preschool, and Jaxie - A short story about a tall giraffe, Koby - The Little blue kagaroo who worried all day. The books are currently part of the London Day School (LDS) Character Education Program, entitled LDS Kind Kids Curriculum ™.

Ms. Lindner is contributor to The Huffington Post and The Alternative Press as the author of Nursery U, a column for parents and educators. She is the mother of two and actively participates in community projects and programs that support and foster the wellness and joy of children in need. She is a frequent guest on TV and Radio discussing various early childhood education and parenting issues, and was named as one of the Top 25 Leading Women Entrepreneurs.

Acknowledgments

I would like to thank my husband & my two beautiful girls who inspire me to write & are always willing to listen to rewrite after rewrite. I would also like to thank my parents for their encouragement & support and the wonderful students and staff of The London Day School who provide so much inspiration for my books. Thank you to Deanna for her support and encouragement during my writing process & of course a big thank you to Justo Borrero who's gorgeous illustrations bring my characters to life.

Made in the USA
Las Vegas, NV
06 July 2022